HAUNTED STATES
of
AMERICA

BEWARE
—→ the ←—
BELL WITCH

D1158480

Beware the Bell Witch © 2019 by North Star Editions, Mendota Heights, MN 55120. All rights reserved. No part of this book may be used or reproduced in any manner whatsoever, including Internet usage, without written permission from the copyright owner, except in the case of brief quotations embodied in critical articles and reviews.

Book design by Sarah Taplin
Illustrations by Maggie Ivy

Published in the United States by Jolly Fish Press, an imprint of North Star Editions, Inc.

First Edition
First Printing, 2018

This is a work of fiction. Names, characters, places, and incidents are either the product of the author's imagination or are used fictitiously, and any resemblance to actual persons living or dead, business establishments, events, or locales is entirely coincidental.

Library of Congress Cataloging-in-Publication Data (pending)
978-1-63163-204-4 (paperback)
978-1-63163-203-7 (hardcover)

Jolly Fish Press
North Star Editions, Inc.
2297 Waters Drive
Mendota Heights, MN 55120
www.jollyfishpress.com

Printed in the United States of America

HAUNTED STATES
of
AMERICA

BEWARE
— the —
BELL WITCH

THOMAS KINGSLEY TROUPE

Illustrated by Maggie Ivy

JOLLY
FiSH
PRESS

Mendota Heights, Minnesota

PAULINE HAASS PUBLIC LIBRARY

CHAPTER 1

MOVING DAY

"What about Watley's Car Care?" Dad asked from the front seat.

Miles Watley kept looking out the window as acres of farmland passed by them on the interstate. It felt like the longer they drove, the farther away from civilization they got. Small farmhouses popped up, sitting on the edges of big fields full of corn and soybeans or whatever else they grew out in the middle of nowhere.

"It's okay," Mom said. "But I think I like Watley's Auto Works a little more."

"The only problem? It sounds like I'm telling people that my car runs," Dad replied, drumming his fingers on the steering wheel. "You know? How is Steve Watley's car? Well, Watley's auto works."

Miles thought he was going to go insane. Through all of Kentucky and to wherever they were in Tennessee, his parents were going back and forth trying to figure out what to call the auto shop. The auto shop that they'd just bought in Adams, Tennessee. Adams, the new town they

were going to live in, was about eight and a half hours from their old house, his friends, and his hockey team.

If Miles had a choice in naming the auto shop, he would've called it the *Thanks-for-Making-Us-Move-to-a-Dumb-Small-Town Garage*. He almost suggested it after the first hour and a half of his parents working on a name, but kept his mouth shut.

"What do you think, Miles?" Mom was turned around in her seat looking at him.

Miles shrugged and glanced at his younger brother, Ryder, who had his earbuds in and was completely immersed in his video game. Suddenly, he wished he'd kept his handheld system out for the drive instead of packed in a box somewhere in the moving truck.

"But did you see what I mean about the one Mom liked?" Dad asked. "If you read it the wrong way, it's kind of goofy."

"No, yeah," Miles said. "I get it."

"What do you think we should call the shop?" Mom asked again.

You don't want to know, Miles thought.

"I'm not sure," Miles replied. "What about something simple like Watley's Garage?"

Mom turned and looked at Dad. They were quiet

for a minute, making Miles think maybe they thought *his* name was stupid.

"It's simple," Dad admitted.

"It's not bad," Mom added.

There! Can we talk about something else now? Miles thought. They'd even turned off the radio to throw name ideas back and forth. Not that he wanted to listen to their old music anyway. But of course, his headphones were packed up and somewhere miles behind them in the moving van.

"We'll have to put that one on the list of contenders," Mom finally said and jotted the name down in her notebook, along with the seven others they were considering.

"Cool," Miles said and turned to stare back out the window.

"So," Dad said after they'd gone another mile or two. "Are you going to stay mad at us forever?"

Miles looked up and saw his dad glance at him in the rearview mirror.

"No," Miles said, but knew the tone of his voice sounded like he was.

"Not sure I believe you, pal," Dad said.

"Well, am I happy we're moving?" Miles asked. "No.

Not even a little bit. I think living out here is going to suck."

"Watch it, Miles," Mom said. "I don't like you talking like that."

"I'm thirteen, Mom," Miles replied. "All of my friends talk that way."

"Well," Mom said, "maybe it's best we're moving away from friends like that."

Ouch, Miles thought.

"It's going to be fine," Dad said, slowing down as they entered a small town. "Just wait and see. A new change of scenery, some new friends—"

"No hockey team for me to play on," Miles said, interrupting.

Dad sighed and nodded slowly, as if he was trying to keep himself calm.

"You're right and I'm sorry about that," Dad replied. "But maybe this is the year you give basketball a try."

"They have a bowling team too," Mom added.

"Perfect," Miles mumbled and stared back out the window.

Ryder tugged at the middle of his earbud cord, making his headphones pop out.

"Are we almost there?" he asked. "I really have to pee."

"Less than an hour," Dad replied, checking the navigation on his phone.

"Yeah," Ryder said, "I'm not going to make it that long."

————————

One pit stop and forty-three minutes later, the Watley family pulled into Adams, Tennessee, the town they were going to call home.

"This is where we're going to live?" Ryder asked, adjusting his glasses and looking at his parents in the front seat. "Seriously?"

Miles wasn't sure what his younger brother expected when the family had been talking about the move for the last few months.

"Oh, you love it?" Dad joked, turning left onto Interstate 41.

"Uh, yeah," Ryder said. "Sure."

He turned and gave Miles a look like he'd just smelled the monkey house back at the Pittsburgh Zoo. Miles gave him a thin smile and raised his eyebrows as if to say, *I told you.*

As Miles stared back out the window, he noticed a bunch of signs along the side of the road. They were white and looked like they'd been there a long time.

Written on one of the signs in fancy old-time writing were the words:

HISTORIC BELL WITCH CAVE INC.

John Bell Cabin

Bell Witch Souvenirs & Gifts

½ Mile

"Did you guys see . . ." Miles began, but the car turned and left the cluster of signs behind.

"Look at these cute little houses along the road," Mom said. "Life is going to be so much more easygoing and calm here."

"Are we going to live on this busy road?" Ryder asked. His face looked pinched, like he was expecting his parents to say yes.

"No, no," Dad replied. "Our place is a couple of blocks off the main drag. But we wanted to live close to the shop, which is farther up the way."

Miles all but forgot about the Bell Witch sign, instead sitting up straighter in his seat to take in all the town of Adams had to offer. They passed some houses that weren't as "cute" as the ones his mom pointed out. Some had a bunch of junk in the front yards or rundown pickup trucks. One house looked like all its white paint was flaking off.

"Hey, there's the fire department," Ryder said. "Wow. It's tiny."

"And that's my cue to turn," Dad said. "Here's our street."

He turned left and headed down the road. As they passed the houses along the way, Miles couldn't help but wonder what the people were like who lived there. *Were there any kids his age? Were there weirdos?* And most importantly: *Am I going to hate it here?*

Within a few minutes, they pulled up to their new home. It was a smaller one-story place their mom called a "rambler" with dark blue paint and a porch along the entire front. A big tree with a weird hole in the front stood close to the road.

"It's kind of small," Ryder said.

"It just looks that way from the front," Dad said.

Miles sat in silence as his dad turned the wheel, making it look as if he was going to drive onto the yard.

"Isn't there a garage?" Miles had to ask.

"No," Dad said, and then laughed. "And I know, I know. It's weird. We moved here to open a garage when my own house doesn't even have one."

Miles looked over at Ryder and his brother shrugged. It felt like neither of them knew what to say or do about what their mom called "their new adventure." Then again, at thirteen and eleven years old, there wasn't much they *could* do.

They got out of the car and walked around. Even though their dad had been there before, he acted like he was just seeing the place for the first time. He pointed out the porch as though none of them had seen it as they pulled up. When they walked around to the back-yard, Miles groaned.

"That's a huge yard," he said. "Who's going to mow it?"

Dad smiled at the two of them.

"Can you buy a riding lawn mower?" Ryder asked.

Both of his parents laughed and they all walked around to the other side of the house. Once they'd finished their orbit, they unlocked the door and went inside. It was empty and quiet. To Miles it felt like an abandoned shell that no one had lived in for quite a while.

"Weird," he whispered.

The only house Miles had ever lived in was their house back in Pittsburgh. It was definitely bigger than this one. *It will seem strange to move all our stuff into a new space*, he thought as he walked across the hardwood floors toward the kitchen. Once through the doorway, he saw a refrigerator and a strange stove.

It was going to take some getting used to.

"I figured out which room I want," Ryder shouted from somewhere else.

"Nice try," Mom said. "That's our room."

"You guys get a bathroom again," Ryder cried. "No fair."

Miles walked over to see which room he was going to get.

"So, here's the bad news," Dad said, looking over at Mom. "There's only two bedrooms."

"One of us has to sleep in the living room?" Miles asked.

"No," Mom said. "You guys will have to share a room."

Miles closed his eyes for a moment, hoping that when he opened them again he'd be back in his own house in Pennsylvania, hours and hours from Adams, Tennessee. The house has a dining room and an eat-in kitchen, but only two bedrooms?! He never had to share a room before.

"That's cool," Ryder said. "Right, Miles?"

Miles opened his eyes. *Nope. Still here.*

"Yeah," Miles said, his voice flat. "Great."

The two of them walked down the hall to where they'd be cohabitating. The room was smaller than his old one back home. It was going to be crowded. It stunk to think that both of them would have to sleep in there. Miles looked out the window and saw it looked out into their big backyard.

"Well, let's bring in what we've got in the car," Dad said, poking his head in. "Then I'll check and see where the moving truck is."

They hauled a few boxes in and set them where they thought they belonged.

"Which side of the room do you want?" Ryder asked when they were back in the bedroom.

"What, are you going to put a line down the middle of the floor or something?"

"No," Ryder said. "I just want to figure out where our beds are going to go."

Before Miles could answer, they heard their dad outside on the front porch, grumbling and saying words that were not allowed as part of their vocabulary. He looked at his cell phone, shook his head at it, then stuffed it into the front pocket of his jeans.

A moment later, Dad came into the house surveying the couple of boxes scattered around. Their SUV could haul a few things, but it was only a small fraction of what they had back at their old house. Mom had told them they would just bring the essentials with them and the movers would carry the rest in the huge trailer.

Dad took a deep breath and then let it out through his nose. "So, bad news guys."

"What? What happened?" Mom asked. She already had her hand over her mouth as if prepared for *really* bad news.

"The moving truck broke down outside of Louisville," Dad said. "They need to get a part. They're not going to be here until sometime tomorrow."

"What about our beds?" Ryder asked. "What are we going to sleep on?"

Miles closed his eyes again.

Maybe it'll work this time.

CHAPTER 2

BRAVING THE CAVE

The Watley family tried to use the few blankets and pillows they had to sleep on the floor of their new house, but it was no use. After a few hours, they gave up and drove to Springfield, the "big" town next to Adams to find a hotel for the night.

Miles lost the coin toss and had to sleep on the small couch in the hotel room. Ryder slept like a king in one of the two full-size beds.

The couch was stiff and smelled funny. Miles lay awake, wondering if he would've had an easier time back on the floor of their new house. He lay on his back, staring up at the popcorn ceiling, dotted here and there with a water stain, and tried to relax.

He knew he needed to change his attitude or he was going to make himself and everyone around him miserable. For the last few years, his parents had been struggling in their marriage and considered splitting up. Both he and Ryder knew that. To leave their old life behind to try something new was a big step for them. He realized that the last thing they needed was for him to shoot holes in everything they were working toward.

As much as the situation stunk, Miles knew he'd try his best not to make it even more difficult for them.

In the beds nearby, the rest of his family slept. Miles closed his eyes and tried to relax. As soon as he felt calm, a car alarm went off in the parking lot outside their room.

"Better attitude," Miles whispered and wrapped a pillow around his head.

———

The next morning, they packed up and drove to the building that was going to soon become *Watley's Whatever-They-Planned-to-Call-It*. It looked like a big metal shed with a single garage door in the front. There was a smaller door to the left of the garage door. The structure was in good shape but didn't seem like anything special. *At least not to pick up and move here for*, Miles thought.

"Here it is guys," Dad said as they pulled up.

"Pretty cool," Miles said, trying to convince himself

of the garage's merit. "I would totally get my car fixed here, if I had one."

Mom turned and smiled at Miles as if she knew he was trying. He, in turn, nodded back as if to let her know he wasn't just saying that . . . even if he kind of was.

They got out of the SUV to look inside the building. It was filled with busted-up crates and assorted junk. It looked like someone had used the big garage as a storage space and then decided they didn't care about all the stuff they'd left there.

"It's going to take some time to clear all this out," Dad admitted. "But we can tackle that after the moving truck arrives, and we get unpacked at home. Today, I've got to meet with the insurance agent to go over some paperwork for this place."

Miles looked around. It was going to take a pretty big dumpster to get rid of all the junky appliances, garbage bags full of clothes, the broken treadmill, and everything else clogging the place up.

"What are we supposed to do?" Ryder asked. "We don't have anything at the house."

He picked up an old baby toy that would make different animal sounds when you pulled the string. It shifted a little and a strange gurgling sound came out of the damaged speaker. He quickly dropped it.

"I know," Dad said. "The plan was to spend the first night in our house and the next day unpacking. But you know how best-laid plans go."

"We could get some breakfast in town and see if we can find something else to do," Mom suggested.

"Sounds like a good plan," Dad said. "You guys go ahead. I'm going to get started on that paperwork. It's the beginning of our new start . . . helping cars start."

"Oh boy," Ryder said. "Wow, Dad. That was bad."

Mom laughed, and Miles smiled. He had to admit, as rough as their move had been so far, it was nice to see his parents happy again. He just hoped it would last.

After listening to Mom unsuccessfully attempt to talk Dad into having breakfast with them, they left and found a small diner farther down 41. They went inside and sat down in a booth with cracked leather seats.

"Good mornin', y'all," an older waitress said, not long after they settled in. "How you folks doing this mornin'?"

Ryder looked at Miles from across the table and raised his eyebrows. He couldn't help but smirk at the lady's accent. She wore a black nametag on her uniform that said ROSE in white letters. It was official. They were down south.

After ordering coffee for herself and orange juice for the boys, Mom picked up the menu.

"You folks visitin' here from out of town?" Rose asked. "Or just passin' through?"

Mom looked at Miles and Ryder a moment before answering.

"Actually," she said. "We just moved here yesterday. All the way from Pittsburgh."

"Well, welcome to Adams," Rose said, her smile even bigger than it was before. "We're just as pleased as punch to have all of y'all here."

Rose took their order and brought their food. As

they dug into pancakes and omelets, Rose came by to see how "everything is tastin' for y'all."

"Is there anything to do out here, Rose?" Ryder asked, his mouth full of pancakes.

Rose gave the restaurant a once-over to make sure no one needed her help, and then motioned for Miles to scoot over. She sat down.

"Well, shoot," Rose said, "I got myself in plenty a trouble 'round here when I was a younger lady. But I suspect that's not what you're lookin' for."

"We just need to kill some time until the moving truck shows up," Miles said. He inched a little closer to the wall. Rose was creeping into his personal space.

"Well, if you feel like takin' a drive, you could go along the ol' Ring of Fire trail," Rose said. "That's kinda fun and educational. There are all sorts of historical landmarks like Johnny Cash's grave, the Bell Witch Cave, and—"

Something inside Miles' head clicked.

"Okay, what's the deal with the cave?" Miles asked.

"You mean y'all didn't see the handful of signs around town?" Rose asked. "It's probably our biggest tourist attraction, but y'all aren't tourists. You folks are local, now."

Miles nodded. It was a weird feeling, realizing that this town was now his home.

"Anyhoo," Rose said, "it's supposed to be haunted. Although I've never seen anything there. There's a whole story behind it, about a farmer and a ghost."

She scratched her big thatch of gray hair with the end of the pencil she had removed from behind her ear. Miles wondered if she ever lost a pencil or two in that wild, forested hairdo.

Miles turned to Mom, suddenly very interested.

"We have to go," Miles said. "Right, Mom? Caves? Ghosts?"

"Are you kidding?" Mom replied. "You want me to have nightmares?"

Rose waved her off. "Ah, it's harmless, honey," she said. "Like I said, I've been there a time or two and I've never seen a thing or gotten myself spooked. The caves are a sight to see, though."

"C'mon, Mom," Ryder begged. It surprised Miles; his little brother was usually scared of creepy things.

"What else are we going to do?" Miles added. "Sit and stare at our empty house until the truck comes?"

Mom took a deep breath, another sip of her coffee, and nodded her head.

"Okay," she said. "But if I get scared, Rose, it's all your fault."

Rose laughed and stood up.

"Ya got it, neighbor," she replied with a wink. "I'll take all the blame."

———————

Just before 10 a.m., they drove their car onto a windy road. To Miles it looked like they were headed onto a farm of some sort. After a few moments they passed through a thatch of trees and found a large red barn sitting on the property.

"There's a cave here?" Ryder asked.

Miles pointed. In large white letters he could see the words:

Welcome to Historic
BELL WITCH CAVE Inc.
FARM

"This must be a mistake," Ryder said. "This looks like the Bell Witch *Barn*."

Mom found a spot to park and turned off the engine. They sat for a moment and watched as an old guy in bib overalls walked around the side of the barn, raised a hand to wave to them, and then unlocked the twin white doors beneath the letters. He pulled them both open.

"Looks like they're open," Miles said.

The three of them climbed out and walked around the dewy grass toward the old guy who stood waiting for them.

"Y'all are here nice 'n' early!" he shouted in greeting.

Ryder elbowed Miles. "I'll never get used to that accent," Ryder whispered.

"You're going to have to," Miles whispered back.

The old guy introduced himself as Clark and got them squared away for the tour. He wanted to wait a few minutes to see if anyone else showed up for the 10 a.m. tour. After a few minutes passed, he shrugged.

"I guess y'all get the VIP treatment," he said. He led them through the barn toward the entrance of the cave.

"Okay, Clark," Mom said. "Shoot straight with me. Am I going to have nightmares?"

"Nightmares, no," Clark said. "But wet feet? Maybe. Also, it's a little cramped in some of the areas. You boys gonna have a problem crouching down a bit?"

"I'm not," Ryder said.

"Me neither," Miles added.

Clark twisted the BELL WITCH CAVE baseball cap on his head as if to tighten it up.

"Then let's go," he said.

Clark led them down a steep set of steps and Miles could instantly feel the air get cold and damp. They reached the bottom step, the ground scraping beneath their feet as they made their way forward.

"So, we're beneath a Native American burial ground," Clark said matter-of-factly as if it were no big deal.

"I already hate this," Mom said and gripped Miles around his left arm, staying close.

Clark pointed out some rules about the cave. He encouraged them to take photos if they wanted to, but no video. Miles found his phone and took a few shots of the passageway. Up ahead was incredibly dark.

As they walked farther into the cave, Clark asked if they'd heard the story of the Bell Witch. None of them had, which seemed to make their kindly old tour guide smile.

"Well, legend has it a man named John Bell bought a farm on this land," he began. "And after a spell, strange things began to happen."

"Like what?" Ryder asked, as if Clark wasn't going to tell them what he meant.

"The family could hear voices and disturbances in the ol' farmhouse," Clark said. "They saw strange creatures 'round the property. Poisonous liquids began to show up mysteriously. They could hear what sounded like an ol' woman singin' Bible hymns."

"Creepy," Miles whispered, but wasn't sure he believed it. He walked ahead a bit, his brother not far behind him, using the flashlight on his phone to light the way.

"Don't git too far ahead," Clark called. He didn't seem too concerned though; he was busy talking about life on the farm in the 1800s for the Bell family.

Miles' feet splashed in a small puddle of water. A drop of water from the cave's ceiling hit him on the back of his neck and he thought he was going to jump out of his skin.

"Holy crap," Miles said. "Did you feel that? Ryder?"

There was no answer.

Miles turned and looked for his brother. All around was darkness with only about six inches of visibility in front of him. There was a small spot of light a little farther back where his mom and Clark were talking.

Did Ryder chicken out and go back? Miles wondered.

"Are you hiding?" Miles cried out. His voice echoed a little off the cave's walls. "You're totally not funny, man."

Still, nothing.

He turned and walked carefully back toward the light

until it got brighter and brighter. When he emerged from the darker part of the cave, he saw his mom and Clark.

But Ryder was nowhere to be seen.

CHAPTER 3

GIRL IN THE DARK

"What do you mean you lost him?" Mom shrieked. Her eyes were wide, and her mouth open in shock. Miles wondered if it was because it would save her time from yelling at him again.

"I was standing right next to him and then he was gone," Miles said. "I don't know where he went!"

Clark walked over and stood between them as if he were a teacher about to break up a fight on the playground. He held his hands up.

"He couldn'ta gone far," Clark said. His voice was calm and as quiet as the darkest parts of the cavern. "We'll find him. These aren't the kind of caves where someone could git lost."

"I just hope he hasn't fallen or whacked his head," Mom mumbled. "I knew this was a bad idea."

They walked deeper into the caves. Miles followed behind Clark, who lit the way with his small but powerful flashlight. They got to the spot where Miles remembered stopping and getting dripped on.

"We were right here," Miles said. "And then he was gone without saying a word."

Clark trained his light toward the left where the path trailed to an opening so small they'd have to crouch to get through.

"Could've wandered off this way," Clark said. "Let's take a look."

As they walked through the passageway, Miles asked, "So why *do* they call this place the Bell Witch Cave?"

"Well, once the witch was done tormentin' the Bell family, it's believed she lived in this here cave," Clark replied.

Clark grunted as he crouched down to duck underneath the rocky archway.

"So, the old woman ran away from their farm and came to live down here?" Miles asked. "If this happened that long ago, she's got to be dead by now, right?"

"Well, that's the thing, son," Clark said. "The Bells never saw an actual ol' woman. Just some strange creatures and mysterious vials. Mostly they were tortured and scared by something they couldn't see."

Miles felt his pulse quicken as Clark lit the way for

him to pass underneath the low ceiling. *What were we talking about?* He wondered. *Some sort of ghost?*

"Watch yer head," Clark warned. "You don't want to bonk it."

Miles helped his mom through the narrow entrance. They had to crouch to keep from hitting the tops of their heads on the low ceiling.

"Ryder!" Mom shouted. "Where are you? Answer us!"

There wasn't a sound except for the occasional drip of water.

"It's possible he found his way to the exit," Clark said. "Some people git afraid of the dark or cramped spaces. You think your boy might have claustrophobia?"

Miles and his mom both shook their heads.

"Well, we'll look ev'rywhere," Clark said. "We'll find him. I promise you that."

Right, Miles thought. *But will he still be alive?*

He shook the thought away, reminding himself that he was jumping to conclusions.

When they got to a fork in the passageway, Miles offered to go to the right while Clark and his Mom went left.

"I don't like this idea," Mom said. "Why don't we stick together?"

"The passage that way"—Clark pointed to the right—"dead-ends to a narrow spot after about fifteen yards or so. We'll just look over here real quick," he said, pointing to the left.

Miles went down the right-hand passage before his mom could stop him, lighting his way with his phone. He had an overwhelming feeling of guilt over losing his little brother in the caves and wanted to be the one to find him.

He glanced behind to see the area where Clark and Mom were standing was still lit.

"Ryder?" Miles called.

"... *here* ..."

Miles froze. The voice he heard didn't sound like his brother's, not even a little bit. It was raspier and airier. He took another cautious step forward, and the scrape of his feet along the loose, wet rocks sounded thunderous.

"Where are you? Quit playing around!"

"... *find me* ..."

Miles gulped hard, feeling his throat tighten. He shined his phone's flashlight in all directions, looking for any sort of sign of his brother or, even worse, the ghost of the Bell Witch.

"*. . . bring me home . . .*"

This part of the cave felt colder than the other sections they'd been in. Miles exhaled. His breath formed soft bursts of mist in the air. He took another cautious step forward, holding the light out in front of him. It barely lit the passage. Up ahead, at the end of the path, was some sort of opening. Something moved across the gap and he squinted to see. For a quick moment he thought he saw a young girl in a green dress.

Suddenly, a hand grabbed him around the ankle.

"Whoa!" Miles shouted, backing away and slamming his back against the cave wall. "What the—"

"It's me," Ryder creaked, huddled up against the opposite wall. His butt was partially in a puddle and the other half on a dry spot. He looked like he'd been crying.

"Dude," Miles said, scrambling down to see him, "are you okay? We've been calling for you. Why didn't you answer? You just disappeared!"

Miles heard footsteps and figured it was Clark and his mom headed their way. At least he hoped it was.

"I got lost," Ryder said, sounding a little sleepy. "My light went out, but she helped me. Do you see her?"

Miles trained his phone's light on his brother's face. He looked just like he did first thing in the morning,

completely out of it. His eyelids were heavy and watery, like he needed to rub them to wake up.

"What? Who?" Miles asked.

"Her," Ryder whispered. He pointed toward the small opening off to his right.

As Clark and his mom arrived, Miles stood and looked in the direction that Ryder was pointing. For a moment, he saw the small girl again before she disappeared behind a rock formation. Though it was hard to hear over the scraping footsteps, Miles swore he heard giggling.

"Ryder!" Mom cried. "Where have you been?"

"He's okay, Mom," Miles said. He saw that his brother was having trouble talking. It was almost like someone shot him with a tranquilizer dart. "He's just kind of out of it."

"I was so scared," Ryder whispered. "But, yeah. I'm ... I'm okay."

Miles and his mom helped him to his feet as Clark kept his flashlight fixed on them.

"He said he saw some little girl down there," Miles said. He pointed to the narrow opening in the rock. "I think I saw her too."

Clark shook his head.

"We git that a lot, truth be told," Clark said. "When some people come down here they think they see some lil' girl wandering 'round."

"Should we look for her?" Miles peered down the cramped tunnel. There was a large crevasse in the middle of the narrow path. It looked about three inches wide, although it was hard to tell because it was so dark.

"No point," Clark said. "We've looked in the past, 'specially in those areas we don't allow folks to explore. No one has ever found anyone or even traces of a person in those sections of the cave. Besides, it's dangerous back there. All sorts of deep holes and pits in the floor."

"So, what was she, then?" Miles asked, almost afraid to hear the answer. "Some sort of ghost?"

Clark shrugged. "No one knows for sure. Some say she's the Bell Witch."

Miles tried to envision the little girl in his mind again. To him, it seemed like she was around six years old. Her green dress had looked old and worn out. He couldn't remember any details of her face. *Did she have one?*

He didn't think she looked like a witch or anything, but just the thought of her looking at him from an almost impenetrable passageway sent chills down his arms and legs.

Ryder exhaled a few times as if he was struggling to catch his breath. Mom kept her arm around him, telling him he was going to be okay.

"Let's get you folks up on outta here," Clark suggested. He led the way out of the cave and they followed.

After a few more tight squeezes and crouching, they reached the exit slope, which led back up to daylight and civilization. Miles watched as his mom made a big deal of breathing the fresh Tennessee air again.

"Thank goodness," she cried. She turned to Ryder, who already seemed like he was back to his old self again. Miles noticed that he looked more alert by the minute. He wondered if maybe his brother just had a panic attack.

Still doesn't explain the voices or the little girl down there, Miles thought.

"I'm sure sorry if y'all got scared down there," Clark said, "but if you did, I'd appreciate you letting yer friends know."

Mom gave him a dirty look.

"Sorry ma'am," Clark said, looking like he was

caught eating the last cookie. "Business has been slow the last few months."

As if to apologize for seeming insensitive to her panic, he offered to show the family the Bell Cabin, free of charge. Miles could see that his mom was about to give the old guy a piece of her mind when her cell phone rang.

"It's your father," Mom said.

She answered and walked away from the group for a moment to talk. As they stood there awkwardly, Clark pulled his hat off his head, smoothed his thinning gray hair beneath it, and put it back on.

"Did y'all have fun?" he asked.

"Yeah," Miles admitted. "It's pretty cool and I like the story behind it."

"Me too," Ryder said. "Even if I did get lost for a few minutes."

"Glad to hear it, fellas," Clark replied. "And the story about the Bell Witch? It's true. There are plenty of books and souvenirs in the gift shop if you're at all interested."

Miles nodded. *Of course there are souvenirs.* He wondered if they had a T-shirt that said: I ALMOST GOT LOST IN THE BELL WITCH CAVE. Miles figured it would be a great gift for Ryder's upcoming birthday. *Or maybe it's too soon*, he thought, smiling to himself.

He heard his mom say something about bad reception below ground. He was sure his dad was wondering what they'd gotten themselves into while he tried to straighten out the garage.

"Okay, perfect," she said. "After the morning we've had, this is probably the best news we could expect."

After a moment she walked over to the group smiling, which she hadn't done in a while.

"Good news, guys," Mom said. "The truck is here."

Clark asked again if they wanted a tour of the cabin and they all politely declined. Miles could tell that Mom wanted to say more to the old guy but held back. He guessed finding out the truck was there at the house had calmed her down and changed her mood considerably.

"Well, then," Clark said with a big smile. "Thanks for comin' on out to Bell Witch Cave. Y'all come back real soon, ya hear?"

As Miles got into the SUV and buckled up, he noticed that no one had pulled into the parking area for the next tour. Miles realized that Clark wasn't kidding when he said that business wasn't all that great.

"Come back soon?" Mom mumbled, looking over

her shoulder as she backed up the car. "Not likely, old timer."

They pulled away from the red barn and drove down the curvy path to the main road. Miles looked out through the back window to see Clark waving at them as they drove off.

CHAPTER 4

DISTURBANCES

When they pulled down their new street and saw the large semi-truck parked out front, Mom squealed. Miles didn't think he'd ever heard her make a sound like that before. The two moving guys who brought all their stuff from Pennsylvania were standing next to the truck, talking to his dad.

"I hope your father is not yelling at those guys," Mom said. "It's not like it's their fault the truck broke down."

Ryder was leaning forward in his seat. No one would have ever guessed that less than a half hour ago, he looked like death warmed over.

"I don't even care about half the stuff in that truck," Ryder said. "I just want my bed back."

"Yeah, nice," Miles said. "You didn't have to sleep on the hotel couch last night."

"Sorry, bro," Ryder replied. "Some guys are just lucky."

They piled out of the car and ran to the back of the truck. The back doors were open and there were boxes piled up in front of all their furniture. Even though Miles remembered watching the movers pack all the stuff in, it still seemed overwhelming.

"These guys are way behind," Dad said, clapping Miles and Ryder on the back after walking over. "So, we're going to pitch in and help. Plus, they're knocking a bit off the bill for getting here late."

The family walked back and forth, up the truck's ramp and back down to the front door, and into whatever room was written on the side of the box they were carrying. They did this over and over. After a while, Miles finally saw boxes with his name on them. As tired as he was, he found a second wind and started grabbing cartons that held his clothes and books.

As he hauled the first box into his room, he saw Ryder setting some of his stuff on the right side of their shared bedroom.

"So, I'll put my stuff over here if that's cool," Ryder said. He waved to the three boxes of his own things he'd already brought in.

"Fine with me," Miles said. He dropped the heavy box with his *Kingdoms of Carnage* books down in his space.

"Looking good, looking good!" Dad said as he hauled two boxes past their room and into the master bedroom.

Miles went back for more boxes and Ryder trailed behind him. As they passed the kitchen, they saw Mom moving boxes around on the counter. She was occupied with getting their things in place.

The brothers moved out of the way as the movers hauled the first of their two couches through the front door. The bigger, older guy was sweating like it was one hundred degrees out. His younger coworker looked like he could've carried the couch on his own.

Miles grabbed one of the boxes sitting alongside the curb and Ryder took another one. They headed back into the house where Dad was repositioning the couch from where the movers placed it.

When they got back to their bedroom, Miles stopped.

"What the heck?" he blurted.

Ryder bumped into him, not paying attention.

"Dude," Miles cried, "watch it!"

Ryder squeezed past him and into the room. When he got a look at their bedroom, he stopped too.

"Hey," Ryder said, "what's going on?"

The two of them looked at the boxes they'd set in the room. All of them were in different places. Miles' box was over where Ryder had placed his stuff. The three boxes Ryder brought in were shoved into the far corner of the side of the room Miles was going to inhabit.

"Dad?" Miles shouted. "Did you move our stuff?"

"What?" Dad shouted from the living room.

"Our boxes have been moved," Ryder said. "We wondered if you shifted them around."

"You guys put your stuff wherever you want it," Dad said. "I'm a little busy right now."

Miles looked at his younger brother, who looked back at him.

"He didn't move it," Miles whispered.

"Well, whatever," Ryder said. "Maybe the moving guys did. To make room for the beds or something."

Ryder went about putting his box down and headed back out for another one. Miles stayed behind and looked down the hallway where the movers were bringing in the end tables and the ottoman for the couch.

They didn't move these boxes, Miles thought. *They haven't even been to our bedroom yet.*

Miles went over to his box of books and set his new box down next to it. As he did, he shivered. He felt a slight chill down near the floor, almost like a draft.

He glanced at the window. It was the middle of August in Tennessee. It was probably somewhere around eighty degrees outside and, considering the windows and doors were open, the air conditioning wasn't on.

"Weird," Miles whispered.

He looked around the room as if he expected to see something that could explain why their boxes were moved. As he did, a slight wind blew through the window, making the old curtains flutter around a bit.

"You're slacking," Ryder said, returning with a lamp and the chair for his desk.

Shaking it off, Miles went back out for more boxes.

———

The Watley family's first full day in Adams, Tennessee, was a long one. Around nine that night, they started to fade. Miles watched his dad fight sleep as they watched the news. Ryder was blinking heavily as he stared at the video game on his phone. Even his mom pulled some deep yawns before she finally cashed out and headed to bed.

Within twenty minutes, everyone else was in bed too. They had another day's worth of unpacking to do in the morning.

Miles came into his bedroom with his toothbrush in his mouth to find Ryder sitting on his bed, staring into his hands. He was rocking back and forth slightly, making his bed creak.

"Dude," Miles said, once he pulled his toothbrush out, "what're you doing?"

Ryder looked up and his face flushed with embarrassment. He closed his hands and shook his head.

"Sorry," he said quickly. "Just kind of zoning out."

"You're strange," Miles said, then continued to brush his teeth.

He walked back down the hall and into the small bathroom to spit. He rinsed once and spit again. When he was finished, he went into his bedroom to find Ryder had already shut off the light. Along the way to his own bed, Miles stubbed his toe on a cardboard box.

"Argh," he muttered. "You could've waited to turn off the lights until I got back."

"Sorry," Ryder murmured from his bed. From the sound of it, he was well on his way to sleep.

Miles climbed into bed and pulled the blankets up over his chest. He lay there in the dark, listening to how different the world sounded in Tennessee. It was much quieter and the bugs making noise out in their backyard made stranger noises than the ones back home.

Back home? You are home now, he thought.

Miles stared up at the ceiling and wondered how long it was going to take him to get used to living in a small town like Adams. It felt like they were out in the middle of nowhere and while it was quieter than living in a big city, the silence was almost deafening.

He closed his eyes to try and sleep. After a night of poor sleep and long day of moving boxes, Miles knew getting some rest was the best thing he could do.

Miles got comfortable and his eyelids grew heavy. Almost as if in a dream (*was it a dream?*), he saw the inside of the Bell Witch Cave. A moment later, the little girl in the green dress appeared and his heart began to beat fast. She was sitting where he'd found Ryder. She was looking down at something. Before Miles could do anything, she looked up at him.

Where her eyes should have been were black empty

pools that seemed to go on forever. Her small mouth was curved upward, in a slight smile.

"... *it's mine* ..." the little girl whispered.

Miles sat up in bed and gasped, wide awake.

What the heck? He thought and looked around. Ryder was still asleep in his bed, lying on his side and facing the wall.

And then he heard it. Somewhere deeper in their house, Miles heard a voice.

He swung his legs off the bed and walked out into the hallway. Moonlight spilling from the open bedroom doors dimly lit the hallway.

Miles moved past the bathroom and felt a strange sensation as if something was going to jump out from the dark and grab him. He moved a little more quickly forward, so that nothing could. When he reached the living room, he paused to listen.

What was that? He wondered. *It sounded like a woman's voice.*

The house was mostly silent. The sound of the refrigerator running was all Miles could hear. He wondered if he somehow spooked the owner of the voice away, realizing how crazy that sounded.

"Hello?" Miles whispered into the darkness. As soon

as he did, he regretted it, worried that someone or something might answer back.

Nothing did.

As Miles turned to go back to his room, he heard a shriek from his bedroom. He thought his heart was going to burst with fear. It took him a moment to realize that it wasn't some sort of monster, but his brother.

Adrenaline kicked in and Miles ran down the hall as the light in his parents' bedroom came alive. His dad burst from the master bedroom just as Miles rounded the corner to his room.

Fumbling momentarily along the wall for the unfamiliar light switch, Miles flicked it on, blasting their dark bedroom with light from the overhead fixture. He squinted as his eyes fought to adjust. When he was able to see a second or two later, he found his brother curled up in a ball in the corner of his bed.

"What happened?" Miles shouted. His dad was right next to him now, and he heard his mom come up behind them.

Ryder pointed to the end of his bed. There, on the floor, were all his blankets. They were wadded up, partially covering a few of the boxes not yet unpacked. At first Miles wasn't sure what the big deal was; he half

expected to see an animal or something hidden beneath the sheet and comforter.

"What are you pointing at, honey?" Mom pushed past Miles and Dad to sit next to Ryder on his bed. As she did, Ryder flinched a little as if surprised.

Miles walked over and kicked at the blankets. They felt cold on his bare feet. He couldn't find anything underneath them.

"Did you have a nightmare?" Dad asked, walking over to the side of the bed. "Was it a bad dream or something?"

Ryder shook his head and closed his eyes in a long, exhausted blink. From where Miles was standing, his brother looked like he was sweating.

"Something . . ." Ryder began.

Miles' mom put an arm around his little brother and handed him his glasses.

"What is it? What happened?" Mom asked, as calmly as possible. She put her hand on his forehead. "Do you have a fever? Is that why you kicked your blankets off?"

Ryder took a deep, shuddery breath before continuing. He opened his eyes but didn't seem to be looking anywhere.

"I didn't," Ryder whispered. "Something tore the blankets off me."

Miles watched in silence as a single tear fell from his brother's right eye and raced down his cheek.

CHAPTER 5

UGLY DOG

It took a while for everyone to calm down. They sat and talked about what might've happened for almost an hour. Ryder insisted that something grabbed the blankets and tore them off his bed. Miles mentioned the voice he'd heard in the dark on the other side of the house.

Everyone was exhausted and after a while, Dad decided that they were just having trouble adjusting to the new place and the big change in their lives.

"So, how'd the blankets come off my bed?" Ryder demanded to know.

Dad shrugged. "Maybe you kicked them off during a nightmare?"

Miles could tell his brother wasn't buying it for a second. The expression on Ryder's face showed that he was upset that no one seemed to believe him; he scowled before tilting his head down.

"The best thing we can do is get a good night's sleep," Dad said. "We're all worn out, guys. It's been a big couple of days and our bodies and brains haven't adjusted yet to the change of living in a new town and house."

Seeing there wasn't much else they could do, both the boys nodded their heads in agreement with their dad. When their parents left to go back to bed, Miles reached over to turn out the light.

"Hey," Ryder said, "can we keep it on?"

Miles didn't say so, but he was glad his brother asked. He wasn't too excited about sleeping in the dark either. Not after the night's events.

"There's something wrong with this place," Ryder said quietly. "It just feels off or something."

"What do you think it is?" Miles asked. "Because I can still hear the sound of that woman talking and it creeps me out like you wouldn't believe."

"I don't know," Ryder said. "But this is just our first night here. What else is going to happen?"

Miles took a deep breath and exhaled slowly. It helped him calm down when he did that. He kept thinking how great it would be to just get up, pack all the stuff he cared about, and take the first bus back to Pittsburgh. He was pretty sure he could stay with Joe or Keith back home.

My parents wouldn't miss me too much, would they? Miles wondered.

"We have to look out for each other, okay?" Ryder continued. "If you hear something weird, wake me up and I'll do the same."

Miles laughed despite how serious his brother sounded.

"You say that like we're never going to get a good night's sleep again."

Amazingly, Ryder smiled back. "No kidding," he replied.

The two of them talked a little longer until pure exhaustion took over. Ryder was the first to drift off as Miles was telling him about some ridiculous video he'd seen on the internet. When he looked over, he saw Ryder was out cold.

"Good night little brother," Miles said.

He reached over to turn off the lamp but changed his mind.

Not long after, Miles was asleep too.

———

The next morning, as the boys shuffled into the kitchen to figure out what to eat for breakfast, their dad stood at the counter pulling groceries out of a bag.

"Got an early start," Dad said. "Figured we'd probably need some groceries."

He plucked a carton of orange juice from a brown paper bag that read "Marty's Market" and had a picture of an overweight bear eating a sandwich.

They sat down for some waffles Dad had already prepared in the toaster and drank some orange juice. Miles twisted his mouth as the taste of citrus mixed with maple syrup. Ryder shook his head at him.

"You think you'd learn by now," he said.

"Can't help it," Miles said as he forked another mouthful of waffle. "I love OJ and I love maple syrup. But they're two great tastes that just don't taste great together."

"Did your blankets stay on the rest of the night, sweetie?" Mom asked.

She sat down and unfolded the newspaper, then warmed her hands around her coffee mug.

"Yes," Ryder said.

"And I didn't hear that creepy old lady's voice again," Miles offered. He realized just then that the voice *had* sounded old. "But the day's still early yet."

"I'll tell you what I think," Dad said. "I think this might be a case of *we-don't-want-to-live-here*-itis. You two think that if you make a big enough stink about this place being haunted or scary or something we'll just

throw up our hands and say: 'You know what? Forget it. Let's pack it up and head back to our old life.'"

"Steve," Mom said. "Calm down."

Dad threw his paper napkin on the paper plate he was eating off of and shook his head.

"I'm calm, I'm calm," Dad said. "I just . . ."

Everyone at the table watched him. After a moment, he coughed into the crook of his arm and sighed.

"I'm tired and a little cranky. And I don't feel

awesome. I just really want this to work. We have to make this all work, guys."

"Dad," Miles said, "we all want it to work too. We're not just saying this stuff to try and get us to move back home. Weird things happened last night and we were kind of freaked out."

"Sorry, Dad," Ryder said.

"Then let's move on, okay?" Dad said, clearing his throat. "We've got a lot to unpack and I need to get the garage cleared out."

Their dad left after breakfast and the rest of them worked on getting the house set up until the early afternoon. Miles had his half of the room arranged the way he wanted. His books were on his shelves and his clothes were back in the dresser and hanging up in the closet. He pulled his hockey gear out and stopped to examine his old jersey and pads.

What am I supposed to do with this?

Miles knew he didn't want to be reminded of how he wasn't going to be able to play hockey at his new school, so he took everything and stuffed it into the back corner of the closet. *Out of sight, out of mind*, he thought.

As he did, his hockey stick fell forward, preventing him from closing the closet door.

"Knock it off," Miles said, fully realizing he was talking to a hockey stick.

He picked the stick up, shoved it back in the closet, and attempted to close the door again. Seconds before he could, the stick fell back down, preventing him from closing the door again.

"Fine," Miles muttered. He grabbed the stick, found a neon orange practice puck, and walked out of his room.

"What're you doing?" Ryder asked as Miles walked into the living room. He was hooking up his video game console to the TV. Near his feet was a box filled with the games they'd amassed over the last few years.

"I'm taking a break," Miles said. He walked through the kitchen, out through the patio door, and into their overgrown backyard.

There wasn't much of a flat surface to play on as grass and weeds had grown into obnoxious green bumps between the patio stones. Even so, Miles found a place to drop the puck. He crouched a bit and snapped off a nearly perfect slap shot. He watched as the puck zipped across the backyard like a neon orange missile. It bounced about thirty yards away.

"All this talent just going to waste," Miles mumbled.

He was glad no one had heard him. They'd think he was a little full of himself.

Miles realized it would be a lot easier practicing with his portable net but didn't feel like digging it out of—wherever it was in this new house. He walked into the yard toward the puck, taking swipes at the long grass with his stick. He kept going until he reached the plastic disc and bent to pick it up. As he did, he heard a growl.

He froze in place, using only his eyes to look around. Something moved near the tall trees about halfway into their yard. Miles squatted down slowly to retrieve the puck. As he did, he heard another strange noise. It sounded like a whimper, followed by a loud, throaty gurgle.

Miles stood up and took a step backward. The bushes shook a little and he saw something black moving behind the leaves and branches. It looked like it was almost the size of a badger. Whatever it was, it growled again. It didn't sound like anything Miles had ever heard before.

"Get out of here!" Miles shouted.

He didn't want some angry wild animal taking over his backyard. When the thing growled again, he lobbed the puck into the bushes. His aim was true, and he heard it thump against the creature.

The animal jumped and scrambled out of the bushes. When it emerged, Miles gasped.

The creature was unlike anything he'd ever seen. It

had jet black hair that covered its entire dog-like body. Its fur was slicked down as though it had just crawled through a swamp. Bright red eyes glowed from what looked like a rabbit's head. One of the ears was bent, as if broken, but the other stood straight up and alert.

Miles was sure Tennessee had different animals than they did back home, but he was pretty sure the half dog/half rabbit beast in front of him wasn't something most people ran into . . . like ever.

He backed up a bit and watched in horror as the monster took a step forward. It extended its snout forward as if trying to catch Miles' scent. When it caught a good whiff, its mouth pulled back into a snarl, revealing its two front teeth. One of them was broken off halfway and jagged, making the creature look even more menacing.

"Back off!" Miles shouted and took another step back. As he did, he remembered he had his hockey stick in his hand. He held it tight, prepared to smack the thing back to wherever it came from.

The rabbit monster growled again and with no further warning, leapt toward him. It closed the distance almost instantly, and Miles swung wild. The curved end

of the hockey stick connected, knocking the beast aside momentarily.

The creature yelped as it fell to the grass and rolled over once, ending up on its back. The dog-like legs kicked, and its torso thrashed as the monster righted itself and was back on all fours again. Miles backed up and saw what looked like foamed milk dripping from its buck-toothed maw.

"Stay away from me," Miles warned the creature. He knew the crazed thing had no idea what he was saying but hoped the smack he'd delivered plus his tone would be enough to scare the creature off.

It wasn't.

The monster bounded toward him and Miles swung again. The force of his swing was so strong, he lost control of the hockey stick and it sailed over the creature's head, leaving him exposed. The rabbit creature barreled into him, knocking him to the ground. Miles landed heavily on his back, knocking the wind out of him. He squirmed violently underneath the creature's weight in a mad struggle to get away.

He could hear the monster's ragged breathing, and a smell like wet garbage met his nostrils.

"Get off me!" Miles grunted.

He shifted his body as the fiend's nasty teeth tried to take a chunk out of his shoulder. Miles narrowly missed getting bitten.

The hockey stick was still held firmly in his grip and he used the blunt end to batter the beast in its side repeatedly. With every blow he landed, he heard it wheeze and grunt. Even so, it didn't seem to weaken or dislodge the creature.

This thing is going to kill me, Miles thought helplessly.

He closed his eyes for a moment and summoned all the strength he could. Using what little energy he had left, Miles swung the hockey stick in a last-ditch effort to free himself.

The hockey stick struck nothing. The weight he felt pressing on him was gone. He could no longer smell the rancid breath the creature emitted.

When Miles opened his eyes, he saw that the creature was gone.

He glanced around the entire yard from where he was lying in the tall grass. He was alone in the backyard, lying on his back, holding onto his hockey stick so tightly his knuckles were white.

Miles sat up quickly, thinking that the monster might jump out and attack him again at any moment.

He listened but heard only the bristle of the wind through the leaves in the branches above him.

He looked down at his arms and shirt. No scratches. No tears. No sign of a struggle. *What was that thing? Was it even real?* He wondered.

He turned around and looked back at his family's new house. It sat there quietly, not looking sinister or dangerous in the least. Even so, something wasn't quite right.

"What is going on here?" Miles whispered.

He wasn't sure, but knew he had to find out.

CHAPTER 6

GIVE IT BACK

Miles burst through the back door and tossed his hockey stick down behind the kitchen table. It clattered on the tile floor, startling his mom.

"Miles!" she cried. "What are you doing? You scared the living—"

"Did you see that thing out there?" Miles shouted, pointing out the open patio door behind him. "That monster that attacked me?"

His mom looked past him and out into the yard.

"What attacked you?" Mom asked, walking toward the patio door.

Ryder came into the kitchen from the living room. He was holding a video game controller.

"What's going on?" he asked.

"Some vicious and weird looking thing jumped at me and tried to bite me," Miles said. "It was like a black dog but had a rabbit's head."

"What?" Ryder asked. His head rolled back on his

neck as if he wasn't expecting to hear what his older brother described.

Mom looked outside from the kitchen but closed the patio door as if to be on the safe side. She tilted her head to try and look along the back of the house too.

"The thing just came out of the bushes and started growling at me," Miles said. "I hit it with my hockey stick, but then it knocked me down. It was trying to bite me and—"

"Where did it go?" Ryder asked. He set his game gear down on the kitchen counter and walked over to where their mom was standing. "Is it still out there?"

Miles sighed, feeling exhausted by everything that had happened.

"It disappeared," Miles replied. "It just . . . disappeared."

Mom turned around and looked at her oldest son. The expression on her face was the definition of worry.

"Did it bite you?" she asked. "Hurt you at all?"

"Well, no," Miles admitted while patting himself down and looking for injuries he didn't know about. "It didn't get me." He knew he wasn't injured and was beginning to doubt the thing he'd seen had been there in the first place.

Ryder looked over at his mom and then back at his older brother. "I'm glad you're okay," he whispered.

"I've never heard of an animal like what you described," Mom said, walking over to Miles to give him a quick hug. "I've heard of jackalopes. They're supposed to be jack rabbits with antelope horns."

Ryder perked up. "Jackalopes? Are those real?" he asked.

"No," Miles said. "They're made up. Some guy thought it would be clever to mount rabbit heads and then put antelope horns on them."

"Weird," Ryder said. "Where'd you see that?"

"On the internet probably," Miles said, which gave him an idea. "Do you have the network set up for your online games yet?"

"Yeah," Ryder said. "Just got done. Why? You want to play?"

"Not right now," Miles said. "I've got some work to do."

Miles went into his bedroom and fished his laptop out of his closet. Knowing the battery was likely dead, he tugged the power cable out too. Clearing a few smaller items from his desk, he made room for his computer and set it down. Once it was plugged in, he powered it up and waited for the operating system to do its thing.

As it loaded, he gazed out the bedroom window, scanning the yard. He didn't see any crazed black rabbit dogs anywhere. Partially hidden in the grass, he saw the orange practice puck he'd chucked at the thing.

His laptop made a noise, letting him know it was ready for action.

Miles sat down at his desk and opened a search window.

I need to find out if I'm crazy or not, he thought.

In the search field, he typed BLACK DOG RABBIT HEAD and hit ENTER.

Immediately, a bunch of results displayed. Most of them described hybrids or creatures from made-up stories. One website that looked like a preschooler had designed it discussed the genetic possibilities of a dog and rabbit crossbreed.

"Not helpful," Miles muttered and went back to the search results.

He scrolled through a few more articles and found fictional stories about demons and monsters, but nothing that seemed to closely describe what he'd seen. As he went further and further down the internet rabbit hole, he found a picture of a jackalope.

"Perfect," he blurted, heaving a sigh of exasperation. Miles realized that he'd gotten a little too far off track.

Ryder came in just then. "What are you doing?"

Miles leaned back in his chair, something his parents reminded him not to do at least weekly. Miles wasn't sure if they were concerned about the chair breaking, him falling backward, or both.

"I'm trying to find the thing I saw in the backyard," Miles replied. "It's not going well."

Ryder sat on his bed. "You think you really saw something out there?" he asked.

"Yeah," Miles replied. "And I didn't just see it, dummy. It attacked me."

"Shut up," Ryder said. "You're the idiot seeing rabbit-headed dogs that just disappear."

The two of them laughed and playfully hit each other.

"Ow," Miles said after taking a punch in his right shoulder. "Knock it off."

Ryder lay back on his bed and winced.

"Hey," Miles said, "you okay?"

Ryder rubbed his ankle and nodded quickly. "Yeah, I'm fine. I just had a pain in my foot."

Miles turned back to his laptop and scrolled down the list again to make sure he didn't miss anything. From what he could tell, there wasn't much to go on.

Maybe I am crazy, Miles thought.

He scrolled back to the top of the page and was about to type in some new search criteria when he saw the IMAGES link. Realizing he had nothing else to lose, he clicked it. As a page of *BLACK DOG RABBIT HEAD* images started to load, Miles gasped.

"Oh wow," he whispered.

Ryder sat up.

"What?" he asked. "What is it?"

Miles clicked on a small image to open a bigger version.

"I think I found it!"

On the screen in front of him was almost exactly what he'd seen. At first, he thought it was an actual photograph of the creature, but then quickly realized it was an artist's rendering of the half dog/half rabbit creature.

It was almost exactly what Miles had seen. The only major difference was the creature's ears and teeth. In the picture on the internet, none of the monster's ears were bent. He also couldn't see the broken, awful-looking

teeth. It looked like it was standing in a field. The artist made the eyes even redder than they'd appeared in real life.

Even so, it didn't look nearly as scary as Miles remembered it. He wondered if that was because the picture wasn't trying to take a bite out of him.

"That thing?" Ryder asked.

"Yeah," Miles said. "Pretty much like that."

"It's . . ." his little brother began. "Really kind of stupid looking."

Miles groaned and held off punching Ryder in the nose.

"I didn't say it was cool or anything, man," he said. "But it was much scarier when it was coming after me."

Ryder leaned in for a closer look. "We should read where that thing came from."

Miles moved the cursor around the screen as if not sure where to go.

"It's like you've never used the internet before," Ryder muttered. He edged Miles out of the way and clicked the link to VIEW PAGE. It opened the website where the image lived.

Almost immediately, the Watley brothers said "whoa" in unison.

"It's talking about John Bell and his family," Miles whispered. "It's the guy that old dude at the cave was talking about."

The two of them read on together. The article talked about how John Bell had moved onto the farm with his wife and kids to start a new life. A short time after they'd settled in, strange things started happening around the farmhouse.

"They heard voices in the night," Miles said, reading the passage while he traced the words with his finger. "It sounded like a feeble old woman reciting hymns."

Ryder turned to his brother, his eyes wide with worry. "Is that what you heard?"

Miles tried to recall what it sounded like. "I'm not sure. I was just a lady's voice, you know? I couldn't really understand anything she was saying."

They read on.

"John Bell's youngest daughter, Betsy, was brutally attacked by the invisible entity," Miles read. "It would pull her hair and slap her."

Both boys were quiet for a moment.

"A ghost can attack people?" Ryder asked. "I didn't think that was possible."

"I don't know," Miles replied. "But you sound like you really believe in ghosts."

"Don't you?"

Miles paused for a second to think. He'd always been told there were no such things as ghosts. But he also knew there were tons of TV shows, movies, and stories about ghost sightings and paranormal activity. There were haunted hotels and pictures of what people thought were ghosts.

And there was the girl he thought he saw in the Bell Witch Cave.

Real or not, Miles just never thought they'd have to deal with a ghost of their own.

"I don't know what to believe," Miles admitted.

They read on until they got to a portion of the article that made Miles read a little faster and louder.

"Early on after moving to Robertson County, which became the town of Adams, John Bell was out inspecting the cornfields." Miles read. "Sitting in the middle of a corn row was a creature with the head of a rabbit on the body of a dog."

"Whoa," Ryder whispered.

"John shot at the thing, but it disappeared before he could hit it," Miles read.

Ryder stood up quickly and looked out the window.

"What?" Miles shouted. "Do you see it?"

"No," Ryder said. "But I wanted to check."

"Don't do that," Miles said. "You're going to scare the crap out of me."

"You mean you aren't already scared?" Ryder asked, sitting back down on the bed. "Because I'm kind of freaking out right now."

Miles shook his head in disbelief. "I don't get it," he said. He turned away from his computer to look at his brother. "We don't live where the Bell family lived. Why would our house be haunted? Why would the stuff that happened to the Bells happen to us?"

"Maybe because we went to the cave?" Ryder

suggested. He shrugged as if he couldn't think of any other reason.

"So, anyone that visits the cave gets a free haunting with their purchase?" Miles said. "That doesn't make sense."

"None of this makes sense," Ryder said flinching, and rubbing his ankle again.

"What's going on?" Miles asked. "Are you okay?"

"Yeah," Ryder said. "I'm fine. I just—"

Just then, farther away in the house, they heard something fall and shatter. Their mom cried out in surprise. Both boys got up from the laptop and ran down the hall to the kitchen. There, they found Mom stooping down to pick up a broken dish. The faucet was running in the sink, steaming up the window above it.

"Are you okay, Mom?" Miles crouched to help pick up the shards.

"I'm fine," she said. "I don't understand how it happened. I was washing the dishes and putting them in the cupboard. The next thing I know . . ." She trailed off, shaking her head.

"Probably slippery," Ryder said. "You know, from the water."

"That's just it," Mom said. "I was already done

with the dinner plates. They were already back in the cupboard."

Miles looked up and saw the cupboard door above them was open. A stack of the remaining plates stood inside, all shiny and clean.

"The cupboard door wasn't even open," Mom whispered.

As he opened his mouth to tell his mom what he and Ryder had discovered on the internet, his heart skipped three beats. There, in the steam-covered window above the sink, was a message scrawled in shaky letters.

It read: GIVE IT BACK.

CHAPTER 7

UNDER THE WEATHER

The front door of the Watley house burst open. Miles, Ryder, and their mom ran out and into the front yard. They scurried across the street and stopped near a quartet of mailboxes.

"What is happening?" Mom cried.

"She wants it back," Ryder said, not sounding like himself. "She wants it back."

"Knock it off," Miles said. "We're all freaked out enough as it is."

Amazingly, his brother didn't snap back at him and instead kept quiet. He clenched his fists closed and open and blinked more often than usual.

"I'm going to call your father and then the police," Mom said, fumbling with her cell phone. Within moments, she had their dad on the line.

Miles looked at the house. From where they were standing everything looked fine. It didn't look like a haunted house and anyone driving by would think it was just a normal, plain-looking home out in the middle of nowhere, Tennessee.

"Steve?" Mom said, calling into the phone. "What's wrong?"

Miles strained to hear what his dad was saying, but it sounded jumbled through the tiny speaker held against his mom's ear.

"Oh no," she replied. "I'm sorry. Come home, then. We need you here anyway. We think there's someone in our house."

Not someone, Mom, Miles thought. *Some*thing. *Some sort of ghost or entity.*

"I don't know, I don't know," Mom replied, moving her hand to cover her eyes. She had just told him about the message on the window. "Weird things are happening. Yes, I'll call them now. And get back here. You sound terrible."

She hung up and looked up the phone number for the Adams police department.

"What's wrong with Dad?" Miles asked. He didn't dare take his eyes off the house for a moment.

"He's sick," Mom replied. "He said his throat feels tight and he's nauseated."

A shirtless guy drove by in a pickup truck, staring at them as he went past. Miles could see that a few of the neighbors they'd never met were watching them from their own front yards.

Great first impression, Miles thought. *The city folk from Pittsburgh are running out of their new house like the place was on fire.*

"This town doesn't have its own police department?" Mom cried. She looked like she was ready to throw the phone into the road in frustration.

"What are you going to tell them anyway?" Miles

asked. "We saw a message written in steam on the window?"

"Yes, no," Mom replied. "I . . . I don't know, Miles. Just give me a second."

From the house behind them, an older woman walked out of her front door.

"Is everything all right?" she asked.

Miles took a deep breath and smiled.

"I think so," he said. "We just got spooked."

The lady fidgeted with her glasses and then looked at the house. She wrinkled her eyebrows as if confused.

"Did the people who lived here before us ever talk about weird stuff happening at the house?" Miles asked.

"Oh heavens, no," the lady said. "The Millers were a younger couple and they just loved their home. They lived there until they outgrew the place after their third baby."

"Okay," Miles said, "thanks. Just checking. Maybe we're just not used to it yet."

"Here comes Dad," Ryder said.

They watched as their dad's truck came driving down the street. He pulled into the small spot in the front yard where there should've been a driveway. All three of them ran over to see him.

Dad opened the door and put a hand out.

"Stand back, guys," he said, sounding a bit out of it. "I have no idea what I have or if I'm contagious."

Dad was pale with a sheen of sweat all over his face. His throat twitched as if he was having trouble swallowing. Despite the warning, Mom went over and helped him to the front door.

Miles stopped and glanced around. It felt like the entire neighborhood was watching them. He almost wanted to shout out: SHOW'S OVER! THE CITY FOLKS ARE GOING BACK INTO THEIR HAUNTED HOUSE! THANKS FOR COMING. GOOD NIGHT!

————————

Since Adams didn't have its own police department, a squad car from the neighboring town of Guthrie was sent over to the house. The Watleys explained what they'd seen, and the officer took a look around. He jotted down some notes and after walking around the property, came back inside. The officer let them all know that he didn't see any signs of a break-in or anything out of the ordinary. Before he left, he handed Mom his card, asking her to call if something else happened.

Meanwhile, Dad was lying in his bed. He didn't come

out for the rest of the day. Not even when it was time for dinner.

"Should we take him to the hospital?" Miles asked from the dining room table. "He doesn't sound good."

"I asked, and he insisted that he'll feel fine tomorrow," Mom said. "He's stubborn like that, you know. The man hates doctors."

It was true. Dad was notorious for saying, "I'll be fine." Whenever he injured or cut himself while working on cars, he would just wrap it up and keep working. If Dad was ever feeling sick, he refused to go to urgent care. He always complained that doctors there would only tell him to drink a lot of water and get a lot of rest.

"If he's still feeling like this tomorrow, we should call someone," Miles said. "With everything else that's happening, who knows what's wrong with him?"

Ryder shifted quickly in his seat just then, startling everyone at the table.

"Sorry," he said, rubbing a spot on his arm. "I just got a little chill."

Miles watched his brother. Like his dad, he was acting strangely. It's had to be seventy-plus degrees in the house. *How was he cold?*

"Ryder and I found something on the internet before

the dish thing happened," Miles said. "The rabbit dog I saw? I wasn't the first one to see something like that."

"What do you mean?" Mom replied. She jammed a fork into her salad, spearing a cherry tomato.

"Remember the Bell family from the cave tour we went on?"

"Oh lord," Mom replied, "how could I forget?"

"That Clark guy said strange stuff happened to their family when they moved into the farmhouse. And the website mentioned a weird creature like the one I saw," Miles said carefully.

"Really?" Mom asked after swallowing a mouthful of lettuce. "You think it's the same one?"

Miles hadn't thought about that. Was it the exact same creature John Bell had seen and taken a few shots at? That was back in the 1800s. There was no way that thing had lived that long. He wondered if the creature he saw was like the Bigfoot of Tennessee. Maybe there were sightings, but no one knew where it came from or how old it was.

"I doubt it," Miles said. "But it's weird."

"This isn't where they lived," Mom said. "Clark said their home was close to that awful cave."

Miles nodded. "That's what I don't get. Some of the

stuff we saw on the website is almost exactly what happened to the Bell family."

"I think she followed us home," Ryder said out of nowhere.

Both Miles and Mom turned to look at Ryder, who was moving his chicken and rice around his plate with his fork.

"Who?" Miles asked. "Who are you talking about?"

"The little girl in the cave," Ryder said. "The one in the green dress."

Miles felt the skin on the back of his neck prickle. The image of the girl he thought he'd seen in the cave and the even creepier one he'd seen in his dream popped into his thoughts.

Was that the Bell Witch? Or did she take different forms?

"I don't want to think about that cave or that little girl," Mom said, waving her hand in the air as if to shoo the thought away. It was almost as if she was afraid to talk about it. "But even if ghosts were real and it were possible, why would she follow us here, honey?"

Ryder shrugged. "She keeps saying she wants it back," he whispered.

The feeling of air being pulled out of his lungs

struck Miles. He looked first at his mom, then his younger brother.

"You can hear her?" Miles asked. "How?"

Ryder stared blankly at the flowered tablecloth, his eyes had an emptiness to them, like he was seeing something else.

"It's like whispers in my ear," Ryder finally said. "But when I look to see who's talking to me, there's no one there."

Mom put her hands over her mouth, as if trying to hide her shock. Her eyes watered as she watched her youngest at the table.

"Can you talk back to it?" Miles asked cautiously. "Maybe tell the voice that we don't know what it wants?"

He was trying to think of anything he could do to help his brother all while not trying to act completely freaked out.

"I tried," Ryder said, "but she doesn't want to listen."

Miles felt his ears ring a bit, reminding him of the sensation he sometimes had after waking from a nightmare. He felt his breath quicken as his heart raced. There was something seriously wrong going on with his brother. It was making Miles both scared and angry.

He stood up, almost knocking over his chair.

"Leave us alone!" Miles shouted into the house. It was loud enough to make his brother jump. He looked like he'd been jolted from a bad dream.

"Miles!" Mom cried.

"This thing, whatever it is, isn't welcome here," Miles said through gritted teeth.

Amazingly, a sense of calm came over him just then. Miles felt as if he'd scared whatever was bothering them away. The heaviness that seemed to be lurking in every corner of the house seemed lighter somehow.

"Do you feel that?" Miles asked his mom and brother.

Ryder nodded and adjusted his glasses. Mom's eyes darted to look around the kitchen, then she nodded too.

Down the hallway, they heard a groan.

"What was that?" Ryder asked, his eyes wide.

Mom stood up quickly. "It's your father."

Miles' stomach dropped.

The three of them abandoned their meals and hurried into the bedroom. There they found their dad, lying in a twisted snarl of blankets. If he was trying to get some rest and feel better, it didn't look like it was working. His dark hair was wet and matted against his forehead. Sweat beaded around his face and his neck was slick with perspiration.

"Steve," Mom cried, coming to his side. "You look terrible! We have to call an ambulance or—"

"It feels like someone slapped me across the face," Dad gasped. "Just as I was falling asleep."

Miles gasped as if he'd been punched in the stomach. *This all sounds too familiar,* he thought.

"Who slapped you, Dad?" Ryder asked. He didn't appear nearly as out of it as he'd been in the kitchen. He looked alert, but also afraid.

"I don't know," he whispered. Then added, "I feel like I'm going crazy." He wiped the sweat out of his eyes and squinted at each of them as if his eyes stung. He rubbed the side of his face as if it still hurt.

"I'm calling the paramedics," Mom said and walked out of the room. "You need to go to the emergency room."

"No," Dad called after her. "Sherry, don't."

It was too late; Miles could see she had already pulled the phone from her pocket.

Miles and Ryder stood by their dad's side. There was no hiding the worry on either of their faces.

"I'm going to be fine, guys," Dad said, attempting a feeble smile. "Really. It might be food poisoning or . . ."

"It's not food poisoning, Dad," Miles said resolutely. "There's something in this house messing with us."

"What?" Dad replied, then gave a weak cough. He looked like he was in pain. "What are you talking about? How do you know?"

Miles took a deep breath before responding.

"Because it's happened before."

CHAPTER 8

PRICKLES

Miles' dad seemed completely confused, even in his nearly delirious state.

"What do you mean it's happened before?" he asked. "What's happened before?"

Miles sat on the edge of the bed thinking how he was going to explain the crazy occurrences. He wasn't sure how he was going to do it without sounding a bit delirious himself.

"I read some stuff on the internet about the people that lived in this area back in the 1800s," Miles began. "The Bell family. They bought a farm and pretty much as soon as they moved into the place, weird stuff started happening."

Dad exhaled a shuttered breath as if he was getting upset.

"What does this have to do with us?" Dad asked. "Did they live here?"

Miles shook his head.

"No," he said quickly. "They lived in a farmhouse

over by those caves we went to yesterday. But they had all kinds of problems. They heard voices, they were slapped, their hair was pulled."

Dad struggled to try and sit up. Miles moved pillows behind Dad so he could prop himself onto his elbows and lean back onto his headboard. "So, what did they say was causing it?" Dad finally asked.

"They called it the Bell Witch," Miles said. Even saying the name they'd given the spirit sent chills down his spine. It almost felt like she was standing behind him, enjoying every moment of what he was telling his dad.

A silence came over the room.

"Every day it got worse," Miles continued. "She started making noises at night, singing hymns. The family even saw weird creatures around the house that some said were the witch taking on different forms. I think I saw one earlier today in the yard. It was a dog with a rabbit's head."

His dad groaned again. At first Miles thought he was in pain or something major was happening.

"I think I *am* getting delusional," his dad croaked. "Did you just say dogs with rabbit heads?"

Before Miles could insist that he really did see that creature, his mom burst in from the hallway.

"I can't get a signal," Mom cried, holding her phone. "I knew we should've had the landline connected!"

"Good," Dad said. "I don't want a bunch of EMTs coming over here and taking me to the hospital anyway. If I can get some rest I'm going to be fine."

"I'm not so sure, Dad," Miles said. "The Bell Witch is messing with us. Just like John Bell's family over a hundred years ago!"

"Miles, let's not talk about this again," Mom said.

"Hold up, Sherry." Dad rasped. "I want to hear what Miles has to say." Then he turned to Miles. "Why? Even if it were possible, why would the witch do it? And how would it get here? This isn't even the same house!"

Miles shook his head and threw up his hands. "I don't know," he admitted. "Maybe it followed us home from the cave."

His dad twisted in his bed as if trying to get more comfortable. It didn't seem to be working.

"Listen to how ridiculous we all sound," Dad said. "We're talking about monsters in the yard, ghosts following us home from some cave, and a witch writing messages on our windows. What has happened to us? This isn't a haunted house! We're just having trouble adjusting to our new life!"

Miles and his mom were quiet. He turned and noticed for the first time that Ryder was no longer in the room with them.

Maybe he didn't want to hear about the Bell Witch anymore.

"Something slapped you, Dad," Miles said quietly. "How can you explain that?"

His dad sighed.

"Maybe I slapped myself in my sleep," he said, nodding. He glanced up at the ceiling and shook his head slightly as if trying to convince himself. "I don't know. I'm not feeling well, and I just need some sleep."

Miles didn't believe it. Not for a second, but he also knew that once his dad's mind was made up, there wasn't any changing it.

"I'm keeping an eye on you," Mom said. "And if you so much as cough or don't look any better by tomorrow morning, I'll drag you to the hospital myself, Steve."

Dad nodded and smiled weakly.

"Fair enough."

Miles stood up and realized the heavy feeling in the house was back again. It didn't seem like shouting at the presence in the kitchen was enough to send it away—at least not for good.

He went into his room to look for his brother but didn't find him there. His laptop was still open and on, but the screen was black, a sign that the power-saver setting had kicked in. Miles touched the pad on the keyboard and the screen lit up.

It was still on the webpage talking about the Bell Witch.

Miles sat down at the desk and skimmed the page, looking for where he left off. He'd been so determined to find something about the creature he'd seen, that he didn't get the chance to read on.

The next section of the story talked about how the Bell Witch became more active as time went on, torturing the Bell family every chance it got. It disrupted their sleep by ripping the bedding from them while they slept.

Miles looked over at his brother's bed.

That happened our first night here, he thought.

He read on and discovered that the ghost interfered with every part of the Bell family's lives. Word spread about the witch's haunting. Former US president Andrew Jackson even came to visit the home to experience the phenomena.

The president believed in this, Miles thought. *Why don't my parents?*

The article explained that John Bell became sick and eventually bedridden. Bell had trouble swallowing and felt like he was being taunted by the ghost, which wouldn't let him rest.

Miles' heart sank as he continued to read.

John Bell never recovered from his illness and died almost a year later. At his funeral, the people who gathered to lay him to rest said they heard wicked cackling and singing for the duration of the service. It continued

until the very last person left the graveyard. After he died, the Bell Witch seemed to disappear. Many believed it retreated to the caves near the farmstead.

"She hated him," Miles whispered to himself. "It's like the only reason she was there was to kill him."

He closed his laptop and sat back in his chair. Just reading about John Bell's fate made Miles feel like his breath was knocked out of him.

It wasn't possible was it? Miles wondered. *Some ghost or wicked spirit could just come and make someone sick? Did this evil thing think his dad was John Bell?*

"This is crazy," Miles said to his empty room. "Dad's going to get better and that's all there is to it."

In the distance he heard murmuring. It sounded like the same thing was being said over and over again. Miles stood up and slowly walked out of his room, pausing every so often to listen. He continued down the hallway until he stood in his parents' doorway.

His mom was curled up next to his dad, who was lying on his back. Both looked like they were asleep.

Good, Miles thought. *They need it, especially Dad.*

Realizing his parents weren't the ones making the noise, he turned around and went back down the hallway toward the living room. The mutterings became louder as he approached. Miles was getting closer to the source.

The light was still on in the kitchen and their half-eaten meal was still on the table. It seemed like hours ago that they'd been there, listening to Ryder talk about the girl in the green dress.

"Ryder?" Miles softly called into the living room. He kept his voice as quiet as he could to keep from waking his parents.

There was no answer.

He didn't know where his little brother had wandered off to and had a quick flashback to when he'd lost him in the Bell Witch Cave.

Miles took another step into the living room. To his left he could see the internet router Ryder had set up. The green lights were flashing as if it were active and online. They illuminated the carpet as if it were a tiny dance floor.

Miles was about to call for his brother once more when he heard the voice.

"... *it back* ..."

He shuddered, and his heart thundered inside his chest. After taking a few cautious steps into the living room, he stopped. Out of the corner of his eye he saw something move. He glanced to his right and caught the reflection of a black shape pass across the dark TV screen.

When he turned toward the window, there was nothing there.

As he debated running out of the house and all the way back to Pennsylvania, an eerie cold wave washed over him. It felt like standing in front of the open freezer door of their refrigerator.

Miles breathed rapidly, feeling panic set in. He almost expected to see his breath in the frigid air.

"*She wants it back,*" a voice whispered from the dining room. "*She wants it back.*"

Fighting every urge he had to scream and wake up the entire house, Miles took three more cautious steps forward. He reached the entryway to the dining room and peered around the corner.

No one was in there.

Someone or something behind him laughed, making his already chilled skin prickle with goose bumps. When he glanced back, Miles saw the living room was empty too.

Of course it is, he thought. *Unless it's a rabbit-headed dog or a little girl, this creepy witch isn't going to show herself.*

Miles' heart was doing a drum solo against his ribs as he took another step.

"She wants it back," the voice said. *"Give it back to her."*

He knew the voice was coming from under the dining room table, but that didn't make it any easier. In a whisper, it kept repeating the same message over and over.

I have to look, Miles told himself. *As much as I don't want to have the snot scared out of me.*

"Give it back!"

Miles got down on his knees and peered under the table. In the center, huddled underneath, was a dark shape rocking back and forth. Its back was to him.

"Hey," Miles whispered, reaching his hand out. An icy chill ran across his neck.

He half expected it to snap its head back and snarl at him. He gently placed his hand on the thing's back.

"Ryder?"

His younger brother turned and looked at him with wild eyes. His cheeks were wet with tears as if he'd been crying for some time.

"What are you doing?" Miles asked, keeping his hand on his brother. "You're freaking me out."

Ryder exhaled, his breath coming out in staggered gasps.

"She keeps poking me, saying she wants it back," Ryder whispered. He looked around as if watching the dining room for someone that Miles couldn't see.

"What do you mean?" Miles asked. "Someone is poking you?"

He grabbed Ryder by the shoulder to try and redirect his gaze. As he did, he saw his brother's right hand tighten into a fist.

Was he going to try and punch me?

"She hurts me, Miles," Ryder says. "She won't leave me alone. She wants it back."

Miles examined his brother closely. He didn't see any blood on his T-shirt or shorts. "Where? Where did she hurt you?" he asked.

Ryder pointed to his bare left ankle with his non-fisted left hand.

With the light coming from the kitchen, Miles saw many tiny dots on his brother's ankle. If he didn't know any better, he could've sworn they looked like pin pricks.

"She prickles me," Ryder said. "But I just wanted a souvenir."

Miles raised his eyebrows in confusion. "What are you talking about, Ryder?"

His brother crawled backward as if trying to get away from Miles. He kept his left hand open to move himself along the carpet.

"What's in your hand?" Miles asked, no longer worried about keeping his voice down. He reached for his brother's right hand, but Ryder snatched it away.

"No," Ryder grunted.

"Give it to me," Miles demanded and tackled his brother. Using his weight and the two years he had on Ryder, he quickly pinned him to the ground. With his free hand, he grabbed his brother's fist and tried to pry his fingers open.

"She'll prickle you too!" Ryder screeched.

"Let go of it!"

With a little more force, Miles opened his brother's hand.

A small, ornate hairpin fell from Ryder's sweaty palm.

"She wants it back," Ryder whispered.

CHAPTER 9

DARK RIDER

Miles picked up the small silver pin and held it between his fingers. The pointy end was tarnished but the top was fancy with loops that formed leaves and flowers. It seemed old.

Really old.

"Where did you get this?" Miles demanded.

Ryder blinked a few times as if he was coming out of a deep sleep. He looked confused and out of sorts, like he'd been taking a nap in the daytime and waking to find it dark outside.

"It was in the cave," Ryder said. "When I got lost, I found it on the ground. She said I could have it."

"Who? The girl in the green dress?" Miles asked.

Ryder nodded his head.

"But now she wants it back?" Miles asked. "This old pin?"

Ryder shrugged his shoulders. "I don't know."

Miles crawled out from under the table, holding the hairpin. It made him feel weird to even have it in his possession. He wondered if it would affect him like it did Ryder.

"We have to get rid of this," Miles said.

Somewhere in the living room came a voice. It was more distinct and clear than any of the mumblings Miles had heard so far.

"O happy home, where thou art not forgotten . . ."

Miles felt a shudder run through his body as a song drifted through the cold and dark house. Despite this, he took a cautious step forward. The floor creaked beneath his bare feet.

"Where joy is overflowing, full and free," the ghost sang softly.

Miles heard his brother scramble out from under the table behind him.

"No, wait," Ryder called. Miles heard him but walked forward anyway. It felt like the hairpin was pulsating in his hand.

"O happy home, where ev'ry wounded spirit . . ."

When Miles rounded the corner, he saw a shadowy figure silhouetted against the window. The dusky sky outside revealed what looked like an almost featureless woman, wrapped in a shawl with her head covered.

She stopped singing her hymn as soon as Miles appeared in the living room.

"You can have it back," Miles said.

He held the hairpin out. His hand shook violently as fear coursed through every inch of his body.

A moment later, the shadowy figure dissipated and formed a dark swirl of fog that arced through the room. It rushed toward Miles and then passed through him. It felt like thousands of icicles pierced his skin. As the cold sensation covered him, an airy, menacing voice whispered into his ear.

"Don't want that, boy," the voice said. *"I want my happy home back . . ."*

And just like that, the cold sensation was gone, and Miles fell to his knees on the carpeted floor. He gasped as if coming up for air after a deep dive into a lake. His breath came quick and heavy.

"Miles!" Ryder cried and ran to his brother's side. He grabbed his older brother by the armpit to help him up.

"She—" Miles stopped as he stood and tried to collect himself. "She doesn't want this old thing back at all."

"What do you mean?" Ryder cried. "What does she want?

"The house," Miles said, his eyes wet and wide with worry. "I think she wants our house."

———

Miles ran into his room and pulled open a drawer in his dresser. He grabbed a pair of socks and yanked them onto his feet. As he turned to leave the bedroom, he ran into Ryder.

"What are you doing?" Ryder asked.

Miles brushed past his brother and went toward the front door. He snapped up his sneakers and pulled them on without untying them first. Ryder, of course, followed him.

"Wait!" Ryder called.

Miles stopped and carefully stuck the hairpin into the front pocket of his shorts. He took a deep breath and let it out.

"I think this stupid old hairpin is the reason this Bell Witch ghost is here," Miles said. "I don't know how or why, but I think she's connected to it somehow. When you brought this thing home, you took her back with you."

In shock, Ryder backed up a step as if the thought he might have brought the Bell Witch unknowingly into their new home was a blow to him.

"It's like she thinks this is John Bell's house and she's up to her old tricks again," Miles said. "Messing with us, breaking stuff, making Dad sick."

Ryder's mouth hung open and his eyes drooped with sadness. "You think she made Dad sick?"

Miles nodded. "She did the same thing to John Bell back in the 1800s," he said. "And he never got better. Only after he died did she go away."

Ryder was silent for a moment, then whispered, "No, no, no. What did I do?"

"I don't know, but I'm giving this thing back to her," Miles said. "Whether she likes it or not."

"How?"

"I'm going to bring it back to where it belongs. The cave," Miles said. "Maybe that will—"

But Miles couldn't finish because as soon as the words were out of his mouth, the house seemed to come alive. Framed pictures fell off the wall, the cupboard doors in the kitchen opened and banged shut. A stack of magazines flew from the rack near the couch like dispersing birds.

"Maybe that's not such a good idea," Ryder shouted, hiding behind the recliner.

It's the best idea, Miles thought. *She doesn't want me to do it!*

He heard footsteps coming and knew he needed to act fast. His parents wouldn't be crazy about him leaving with it getting dark outside.

"What's going on out there?" Mom called frantically from the hallway.

Miles grabbed the doorknob to the front door and pulled it open. Almost immediately, it slammed shut again.

"Knock it off!" Miles shouted and grabbed the doorknob again. It was icy cold in his hand. Ignoring the sting, he yanked the door open so wide it banged against the wall. Before the witch could react, he ran out and into the front yard.

As expected, the door slammed shut behind him. He looked back to see his brother watching him through the front window.

Don't tell Mom what I'm doing, Ryder, Miles thought. *I can't have her trying to stop me.*

Miles ran around the side of the house to the storage shed. As he did, a lawn chair from their front porch flew off and into the yard. A potted plant fell from its perch and smashed onto the sidewalk.

"Keep moving," Miles whispered to himself. He grabbed the shed's door handle and flung it open. A rake flew from inside and grazed his shoulder. All around him he heard a high-pitched, cackling laugh.

Without slowing down, Miles grabbed his bike and pulled it out of the shed. Its pedal got caught on the lawn mower. As he struggled, a bin full of water guns fell from the top shelf, clattering down on the floor around him.

Nice try, Miles thought as he wrenched his bike free.

He turned his mountain bike so that it was facing the road and did a running mount. With the momentum from his mount, he rode through the long grass and onto the street. Mailboxes burst open and the ones with mail in them belched envelopes and letters all over the road.

"Miles!" his mom shouted from the front yard.

"Stay with Dad and Ryder!" Miles shouted over his shoulder. "I'll be back!"

When Miles turned his attention back to the darkening road, he saw a small, rusty wagon barrel on the street and in his path. He swerved, narrowly missing it.

He raced down the road, watching as random objects were thrown in his direction. He didn't realize until just then how dark the streets were in Adams. The fading sunset and the lack of street lights in his neighborhood gave him little visibility. Most homes were lit up, and inside people with normal lives were eating dinner or watching TV.

A basketball clipped his front tire and he nearly lost control of his bike.

Lights, he thought. *Lights would be good here.*

He clicked on the battery-powered light affixed to the handlebars. It had been forever since he'd used it and wasn't sure the batteries were any good. Miles almost cheered when the bulb lit up nice and bright.

"Now we're talking," he whispered. As he approached the fire station on the main road, he turned right, riding along the shoulder of Interstate 41.

His legs pumped hard as he rode along as fast as he could. Sweat formed above his brow and he used his hand to quickly wipe it away. The lights along the main road blinked off as he passed beneath them. The closer Miles got to the Bell Witch Cave, the more he realized he was on the right track.

She definitely didn't want him—or maybe the hairpin—to go back there.

To make sure he hadn't lost it, Miles patted his front pocket. The hairpin was still there. Miraculously, the witch hadn't given him any "prickles" yet. She was too busy trying to stop him from getting to the cave.

Miles glanced back over his shoulder to look for cars before crossing the highway. For a moment, he thought he could see a shadowy figure lumbering after him. Just to be safe, he pedaled a little faster.

His handlebar light illuminated a cluster of white square shapes along the side of the road. As he got closer, Miles could see that they were the Bell Witch Cave signs he'd seen on the day they'd arrived in Adams.

As he neared the corner and his next turn, a transformer on the electrical pole across the street sparked and exploded, casting an orange light over the intersection. The blast made Miles swerve into the ditch where he almost smashed into the signs on the corner.

She is not messing around! Miles thought, as panic rose into his throat. He turned his bike back toward the

road and made the left. According to the sign, he was only a half mile away from the cave.

He tore down Keysburg Road, standing up on his pedals to give himself as much speed as possible. An old picket fence along the right side of the highway lined the property of a school. Weather-worn boards creaked and snapped loose from their posts and launched themselves at Miles and his bike. They clattered against his bike frame and legs, but thankfully not causing any damage or injury.

"Just have to keep going," Miles told himself.

He glanced over his shoulder. Other than the fire from the electrical transformer farther back, the road was dark.

After what seemed like thirty miles and not just half of one, Miles saw the familiar white sign. It directed him to turn right and listed the months that they were only open on the weekends. Behind that was a red sign touting:

BELL WITCH CAVE CANOE RENTAL — May thru Sept.

As Miles rounded the corner, the signs shook on their posts, but stayed intact. He wondered if the witch wasn't strong enough to rip the signs from the ground.

She just made a light pole explode, Miles reminded himself. *Don't underestimate her!*

Then something caught his eye that made him jam on the brakes.

Next to the sign that reminded visitors that alcohol, profanity, pets, and video cameras were strictly prohibited, was a gate. A locked gate.

Miles stopped and felt his exhaustion settle in. There was no way he was going to get through the gate, at least not on his bike. He hopped off his bike and jogged it over to the twin gates, cinched in the middle with a rusty chain and an aged lock.

While he was sure he'd be able to squeeze through the fence or gate without any problem, he didn't want to walk the rest of the way. He twisted his handlebars to the right and illuminated the wood fence that enclosed the property too.

Maybe I can't go through the gate, he thought, *but I could go over it.*

He quickly jogged his bike up the slight hill near the wooden split-rail fence. Using some effort, he lifted his bike up and over the wood. As he did, the big metal gates groaned and shook in protest.

Miles set his bike down on the other side. As his feet hit the ground, the SPEED LIMIT 10 MPH sign snapped loose and launched at him. It narrowly missed his leg.

The sign's sharp corner struck the wooden fence and stuck there like a ninja's throwing star.

"That was too close," Miles gasped.

He quickly righted his mountain bike and readjusted the light on the handlebars. With a running start, he mounted his ride again and tore off down the dirt road, heading for the Bell Witch Cave.

CHAPTER 10

HEADING HOME

Miles followed the curved road, using the small light from his bike to guide the way. Gravel popped and shot out from beneath his tires as he followed the sunken wheel ruts in the dirt. As he passed beneath the trees, he heard laughter in the wind.

"You're not scaring me," Miles cried into the dark. Truth be told, he was terrified.

Finally, his light illuminated the white letters on the red barn. The words BELL WITCH stood out, almost as if giving Miles one last warning.

He rode up to the closed white door and set his bike down near the giant oak tree.

It was dark and the only sounds he could hear were his heart beating and the creak of the barn doors being blown on their hinges.

Miles walked away from his bike and looked at the locked doors. A simple padlock held them closed. Thankfully, there was a gap between the door and the ground that he was almost positive he'd be able to squeeze under.

It is going to be dark in there, he realized and patted the front pocket of his shorts. The hairpin was there, but his cell phone wasn't. In his rush, he'd left it at home. He didn't have a flashlight.

He turned and looked at his bike. The light on the handlebars was still nice and bright.

"Well, there you go, dummy," Miles whispered.

He ran to his bike and grabbed the light. It was held in place with a clamp that his dad helped him affix with a screwdriver. Since there was no way to be careful about it, Miles ripped the light from the bracket, snapping the plastic.

He breathed a sigh of relief to see that it still worked.

"Stay away . . ." a voice whispered in the wind. Even though he was sweating through his T-shirt from his ride, Miles felt a chill race through him.

He scrambled to the door and set the light down near the barn door's gap. Miles got down on his belly before he could talk himself out of it. He army-crawled beneath the old wooden doors, the rough edges of the planks digging into his back. It was a tight squeeze.

He quickly stood up and grabbed the light from the ground before the witch could.

The wind made the barn creak and groan as if having Miles inside was giving it a stomachache. He took a few cautious steps forward, heading toward the steep wooden staircase that led down into the caverns.

He peered down the stairs and even with his bike light, the darkness seemed thick enough to swim in.

Here goes nothing, Miles thought and descended into the cave.

The air was damp and heavy at the bottom of the steps. The sound of dripping water came from farther off in the cave. He swung the light to his left and right, hoping beyond anything that he wouldn't find someone or something else down there with him.

What looked like a howling face peered back from the dark, making Miles take a quick step back. As he looked a little more closely, he saw it was a just a trick of the light and shadows on the rock formations.

"Keep it together, Miles," he whispered to himself. "It's just a cave. Just a dark, damp, haunted cave."

He kept going until he found the spot where Clark, his mom, Ryder, and he were separated. Just ahead was the passage where he had to crouch down so he didn't bump his head on the rocks above.

"I've got you now . . ."

Miles ignored the voice, but the light in his hand started to switch on and off. He felt cold drafts brush past and through him as he pushed on into the darkness.

Almost there, Miles thought. He didn't know if it mattered, but he wanted to bring the hairpin back to where he'd found his brother curled up on the ground. He put his hand up to the ceiling, touching something wet.

"Gross," he whispered. Miles held his hand in front

of the light. He was relieved it was only water and not something worse.

Like blood.

He reached the fork in the cave where he'd lost Ryder. Aiming his light down the right-hand passageway, he saw the tunnel snake off into the darkness. As Miles headed in that direction, he reached into his pocket and found the hairpin.

It felt as cold as ice between his fingertips.

Deeper in the cave he heard soft laughter and footsteps. The wind picked up, spraying tiny droplets of water from the puddles on the floor onto his bare legs, arms, and face. He wiped it away and kept moving.

Up ahead, he could see a small face peering out at him from around a corner.

"I'm bringing it back, whether you want it or not," Miles said, hoping she knew he meant it. His voice sounded small and unsure as it echoed through the caverns.

The little girl in the green dress smiled slightly before she turned to run down the path. In seconds, she disappeared into the dark.

Just then, he felt a heavy hand come to rest on his shoulder. It felt like it was carved out of ice and the fingertips seemed to sear his skin through his T-shirt. His whole body felt cold and stiff as if he were slowly freezing solid.

Miles jerked away, then spun around and shouted, "Leave me alone!"

His voice was loud and powerful as it echoed through the damp cavern. He felt the presence of the ghost withdraw into the black throat of the cave. It was gone, but Miles knew it would be back. He couldn't waste another moment. It was time to give the old hairpin back to the witch.

Miles picked up his pace, continuing down the passageway until he found the spot where Ryder had ended up. Written in the dust on the ground was the word HOME.

Over and over and over.

She really wanted her home back, Miles thought. *No matter who the house belonged to.* He just hoped that by bringing the hairpin back, she'd stay away from his home.

He walked over to the opening where he'd seen the little girl for the first time. The passageway was in poor condition. Clark had warned them that there were all sorts of pits and weak spots in the floor.

Miles shone his light inside the tunnel, spotting a large, dark crack running along the side of the wall.

It would have to do.

He carefully climbed over the rock wall and through the opening. Cautiously, he tapped the ground near the crack. It seemed strong enough to hold him. As he squeezed himself into the cramped space, out of the corner of his eye he saw a shadow move along the stone wall, but he ignored it.

He held the hairpin up over the crack in the floor. The light glinted off the tarnished metal momentarily, making Miles squint.

"No . . ." the witch hissed from deeper in the dark. *"I want what is mine!"*

"This is yours," Miles said and dropped the hairpin. "But you're not taking our home!"

As the antique hairpin fell, he saw a small, child-like hand reach up from the crack as if to catch it. The hairpin slipped through its fingers and fell into the deep darkness.

He watched as the hand closed shut as if it had caught the relic, then disappeared.

Almost immediately, the heaviness and the cold he'd felt since taking the pin was lifted from him.

Miles listened to hear the hairpin clatter against the rocks somewhere far beneath the cave, but the sound never came. It didn't matter. The cursed thing was gone and no one else was going to pick it up. He just hoped it also meant the Bell Witch was gone forever.

———————

Miles rolled into his front yard twenty minutes later, completely exhausted. He hopped off his bike and let it fall, too tired to bother with the kickstand.

He barely got to the porch when the door flew open and his mom and brother ran out.

"Miles!" Mom shouted. "Where have you been? You look terrible!"

Miles looked down at himself. His T-shirt was filthy and soaked with sweat. There was dirt on his knees and arms. He could tell his hair was a wet, sloppy mess.

"Yeah," he said. "I guess I do."

"Where did you go?" Mom demanded. "I was just about to call the police to start searching for you."

Miles explained how Ryder had picked up the hairpin when they visited the Bell Witch Cave. He told his mom that it somehow brought the entity that haunted the Bell family (and all her various forms) to their house, and how all of the weird things happening to them were similar to what happened to the Bells in the 1800s.

"So I had this idea that if I brought the dumb thing back to the cave, the ghost would follow me," Miles said.

"Did it?" Ryder asked.

"You could say that," Miles replied, nodding.

"I'm starting to think you guys watch too many movies," Mom said.

"So, is she gone?" Miles asked, looking at his brother. "The witch, I mean?"

Ryder nodded. "I think so," he said, smiling for the first time in a while.

Miles exhaled a sigh of relief.

"What about Dad?" Miles looked at the house in worry. He knew what had eventually happened to John Bell way back when.

"Sound asleep," Mom said, smiling.

———

The next morning, Miles could feel something grab his ankle. Before he could open his eyes, he assumed the worst.

It was the Bell Witch!

He sat up and looked to see his dad standing over him.

"Seriously," Dad said. "I was beginning to think you were going to sleep all day."

Miles rubbed his eyes and glanced around the room. It was bright and sunny outside. Ryder's bed was empty.

"What time is it?"

"Almost eleven o'clock," Dad said. "You hungry for breakfast or lunch?"

"Very funny," Miles said and then realized something. His dad wasn't bedridden anymore. "Are you feeling better?"

"Much better," Dad replied. "Like a crisp one hundred-dollar bill."

Miles sat up and looked his dad over. His appearance was like night and day. The dark circles were gone from under his eyes, the color returned to his cheeks, and he seemed completely alert. He didn't look anything like the zombie he'd turned into just the day before.

"Wow," Miles whispered. "It really worked."

"Of course it worked," Dad said. "I told you I just needed some sleep." He squeezed his ankle one more time. "Come out to the kitchen when you're ready. We've got stuff to talk about."

"Like what?" Miles asked, suddenly a little more

awake. *Moving back to Pittsburgh? Actually, this place isn't so bad.*

"We need to finalize the auto shop's name," Dad said with a bright smile. "And I'm sure you've got some great ideas."

Miles groaned and lay back down on his pillow. *Not this again. This conversation would've been enough to drive the Bell Witch away!*

AUTHOR'S NOTE

Beware the Bell Witch was definitely a tricky story to write as there are so many different elements to the creepy story and legend. The ghost known as the Bell Witch was said to do things that ranged from mean and scary to downright murderous.

What stuck out to me was that according to the legend, the ghost actually inflicted harm on the Bell family back in the 1800s. Ghosts aren't supposed to be able to harm the living, but this one is said to have done so. The witch slapped and pulled hair. She seemed happy to do it, based on how often the family could hear her laughing. It's believed the Bell Witch was also responsible for John Bell's death by poisoning him. Small vials of a mysterious liquid were found around the Bell farm. A doctor tested it by feeding it to the family cat and it died almost instantly. They destroyed a vial, but some wonder if John had somehow ingested the liquid and that's what made him sick.

The legend isn't clear as to why the ghost hated John Bell so much to want him dead. In my opinion, that's one of the scariest things about the story. In this book I tried to make it seem like she really didn't like Miles' dad, either. I just wanted to make sure Miles figured out what to do in order to keep his dad alive to prevent the legend from repeating itself!

In reading up on the legend, I was curious about why the ghost was known as the Bell "Witch" and not the Bell "Ghost." It turns out, around that time in the 1800s, people thought that any strange or paranormal happenings were considered witchery. The Salem Witch Trials happened in 1692, so the idea of "witches" was likely something people from that time period still talked about.

Yes, the Bell Witch Cave is a real place, but I had to use research and some creativity to describe it since I'd never been there. Some claim to have seen a small girl in a green dress in the Bell Witch Cave. Is it the Bell Witch when she was young? If you ever have a chance to go to Adams, Tennessee, you should stop and find out!

ABOUT THE AUTHOR

Thomas Kingsley Troupe has been making up stories ever since he was in short pants. As an "adult," he's the author of a whole lot of books for kids. When he's not writing, he enjoys movies, biking, taking naps, and investigating ghosts as a member of the Twin Cities Paranormal Society. Raised in "Nordeast" Minneapolis, he now lives in Woodbury, Minnesota, with his awe-inspiring family.

ABOUT THE ILLUSTRATOR

Maggie Ivy is a freelance illustrator and artist who lives and works in the Ozark area in Arkansas. She found her love for art at an early age and pursued it with passion. She graduated from The Florence Academy of Art in 2010. She loves narrative elements and story-building moments, and seeks to implement them in her own work.

A MINNESOTA GHOST STORY

City-boy Robby Warner is spending the Fourth of July holiday in the small town of Hibbing, Minnesota, where the only thing that's happening is his large, chaotic family reunion. It isn't long before he and his cousins decide to escape the crowd to explore all that the town has to offer. But while visiting an outdated bus museum, strange things start to happen, like bus windows closing on their own. When Robby plays back a video he took at the museum, he hears a ghostly voice whisper to him. The ghost is looking for something he'd lost. Will the ghost find what he's looking for, or will he keep searching for eternity?